BATTLE BUGS

THE SPIDER SIEGE

NO LONGER PROPERTY OF ANYTHINK LIBRARIES/ RANGEVIEW LIBRARY DISTRICT

D1015983

by JACK PATTON
illustrated by BRETT BEAN

SCHOLASTIC INC.

With special thanks to Adrian Bott

If you purchased this book without a cover, you should be aware that this book is stolen property. It was reported as "unsold and destroyed" to the publisher, and neither the author nor the publisher has received any payment for this "stripped book."

Text copyright © 2015 by Hothouse Fiction.
Cover and interior art by Brett Bean, copyright © 2015 by Scholastic Inc.

All rights reserved. Published by Scholastic Inc., *Publishers since 1920.* 557 Broadway, New York, NY 10012, by arrangement with Hothouse Fiction. Series created by Hothouse Fiction.

The publisher does not have any control over and does not assume any responsibility for author or third-party websites or their content.

SCHOLASTIC and associated logos are trademarks and/or registered trademarks of Scholastic Inc. BATTLE BUGS is a trademark of Hothouse Fiction.

No part of this work may be reproduced, stored in a retrieval system, or transmitted in any form or by any means, electronic, mechanical, photocopying, recording, or otherwise, without written permission of the publisher. For information regarding permission, write to Hothouse Fiction, The Old Truman Brewery, 91 Brick Lane, London E1 6QL, UK.

This book is a work of fiction. Names, characters, places, and incidents are either the product of the author's imagination or are used fictitiously, and any resemblance to actual persons, living or dead, business establishments, events, or locales is entirely coincidental.

ISBN 978-0-545-70742-8

12 11 10 9 8 7 6 5 4 3 2   15 16 17 18 19 20/0

Printed in the U.S.A.   40
First printing 2015
Book design by Phil Falco and Ellen Duda

CONTENTS

CAMPING TRIP

Max Darwin lifted the glass lid of his brand-new bug tank and dumped in some fresh cucumber slices. "Here you go, Millie! Enough to last you through the weekend!"

Millie, his new pet millipede, nuzzled her way out of the moss she was hiding in and inched over to enjoy the food. Max grinned, bending over so he could watch her.

She is so cool! he thought. Max loved the way her long, segmented body seemed to glide over the hills and valleys of her little kingdom, her horseshoe-shaped feelers waving in front of her. It was amazing how her dozens of tiny legs worked together in total harmony.

In the next tank over, his walking sticks clambered around their own mini-jungle. Max made sure they had plenty of food, too.

"Max! I said it's time to go!"

Max sighed. "Coming, Mom! I'm just making sure the bugs are okay."

He gave Millie a longing look, wishing there was time to lift her gently out of her tank and let her crawl over his hands.

"I'll be back soon, guys, okay?" he told his roomful of insect friends. "You all have plenty to eat, so don't eat each other!"

"MAX!"

He bounded down the stairs two at a time. The front door was open. His mom waited outside, arms folded.

Max got as far as the doormat, then did a one-eighty-degree turn and ran back inside. "Forgot something!" he yelled over his shoulder.

He ran to the kitchen, then back to the living room again. *Where is it? How could I lose something so huge . . . ? Aha!* Max found it propped open on the dining room table, right where he'd left it. The leather-bound *Complete Encyclopedia of Arthropods* was more than just a book. It was the gateway to a hidden, magical realm. He quickly checked that the magnifying glass was still tucked into the inside front cover pocket.

"Can't go anywhere without this," Max said to himself. He stuffed the encyclopedia deep into his backpack and zipped the zipper so it wouldn't fall out.

In the driveway, the family RV's motor was already running. Behind the wheel, Max's dad was making a big show of looking at his watch. "Good to see you, son. I thought your bugs might have eaten you alive."

"Very funny, Dad!" Max climbed in and fastened his seat belt.

His mom got in front. "You'd better not have any beetles in your pockets," she said as she buckled up.

Max snorted. "Right, Mom."

He didn't bother to tell her *why* he didn't have any: smuggling beetles in his pocket would be cruel—grown-ups didn't always understand stuff like that. All too often, they thought that liking bugs was weird.

"Engaging main rocket drive!" Max's dad said, putting the RV into gear while Max's mom rolled her eyes. Max fidgeted with excitement as the big vehicle reversed out onto the main road and sped away. The open road, and the promise of a whole weekend of bug-hunting fun, lay ahead.

Max knew the journey to the Wildgrove Acres Campsite would take hours, but he couldn't wait to get there. The forest would have so many new bug species to explore!

His dad put on his favorite pop music radio station. His mom switched it to a rock station. His dad switched it back. As they playfully struggled, Max closed his eyes and let his thoughts drift away.

The musty, mysterious old bug encyclopedia that his mom had found in the library of an old mansion had turned out to be a gateway to another world. He'd been shocked to find himself looking through its magnifying glass one minute, and shrunk down to bug size the next. Even more shocking were the friends he'd made on tropical Bug Island—talking insects, arachnids, and other mini-beasts. The only problem was that their home was under threat from invading reptiles.

However, with Max's human-size brain on their side, the tide had quickly turned. He'd come up with new ways to fight the enemy and hatched a clever plan when the bugs were in danger of being wiped out by lizard forces. General Komodo, the reptile leader, had been furious.

Max yawned. He wondered where Spike, Webster, Buzz, and Barton were now. How were the Battle Bugs doing without his help? He'd tried to use the magnifying glass again to enter their world, but it hadn't worked. As he leaned his head against his car seat and began to doze off, he wondered if he'd ever see Bug Island again.

Three hours later, Max jolted awake. The RV was slowing down. He rubbed his eyes and saw that they'd made it to Wildgrove Acres!

"You slept through the whole trip!" his mother told him. "I wish I had that talent."

His dad took a deep sniff. "Smell the air—that's nature! Pure and clean and good for you."

He parked the RV in a shady spot, and

they all jumped out. The forest surrounded them. It was surely a treasure trove of insect life. Max could almost feel it pulling at him, like an ache in his bones.

"Can we go and look for bugs?"

"We just got here!" His dad laughed. "Lunch first. The bugs can wait."

"But, Dad!" Max pleaded. There would be bugs nesting in the fallen leaves, scrambling up the branches and twigs, burrowing under the bark, lurking in rock piles, and feasting on fallen fruit. How was he supposed to think about *lunch* at a time like this?

His dad gave him a stern look, but only for a moment. "Well, all right, buddy. Let's go."

They eagerly headed into the forest. Max found a grasshopper, a katydid, and two ladybugs within minutes. He pointed out the katydid's long antennae to his father, who'd thought it was just another grasshopper. "Easy mistake," Max said, grinning.

Then he spotted a flash of gold between two big boulders. Breathlessly, he leaned in close. It was a giant spiderweb made of golden-yellow silk!

"What kind of spider could have made this?" he whispered. "I've never seen anything like it!"

As if introducing itself, the spider came running up one of the gleaming strands.

It was nearly two inches across, a deep reddish color with bright, green-yellow markings. Max jotted down a quick description and began running back toward the RV.

"You can't be finished already," his dad said in confusion.

"I need to look up that spider!" Max yelled back.

Alone in the motor home, he pulled out the encyclopedia. He flicked through the pages, searching for the entry on spiders. But before he could even turn to the arachnid section, he heard a faint buzzing coming from inside the book.

That's what happened last time I got

called to Bug Island, he thought excitedly. *I bet the bugs need my help! Maybe I can get back there!* Suddenly, all thoughts about the spider disappeared, and he quickly turned to the double-page section on Bug Island.

Wait. Max had to make sure he was alone. Through the small window he saw his parents digging a little pit; it looked like they were making a campfire. *Great, they'll be busy with that forever.*

He pulled out the magnifying glass. Peering closely, he could just make out Buzz, the giant hornet!

Suddenly, the world began to spin, and he had the sensation of being pulled through the magnifying glass. He felt dizzy and a little bit sick.

"Here we go again," he whispered.

The pages of the book rushed up toward him. He was being drawn in . . . back to Bug Island!

BACK TO BUG ISLAND

Max landed with a thump on Bug Island. The blades of grass around him were the size of broom handles, and the trees towered above as high as skyscrapers. Once again, he'd shrunk down to bug size.

He picked himself up and looked around. He was standing on top of a hill that bulged up from the woods like a lookout post.

Where was Buzz? Max couldn't see a sign of her anywhere. Had he landed on the wrong part of the map? Or was he just too late to help?

He had to find out why Buzz had called him through the encyclopedia. He looked out across the landscape. There was the Reptilian Empire, a dusty, sandy island rising out of the sea. And there was the grayish-black rock bridge that now connected it to Bug Island.

The bridge was brand-new, made from cooled-down lava that had flowed from an erupting volcano. Bug Island, which had been safe from the reptiles for years, was now under constant attack. The reptiles could slither, scuttle, and crawl across the rock bridge and eat their fill.

Or they would have, if not for the heroic Battle Bugs. Max was sure they must be on duty somewhere, protecting Bug Island. He continued his survey of the landscape. Down the hill, in the middle of the forest, he saw what looked like a clearing. There were mounds, earthen walls, and little shapes crawling back and forth among them.

The Battle Bug camp! he guessed.

Although there were no reptiles in sight, Max felt anything but safe. If that really was the bug camp down there, he needed to get to it as fast as he could.

He set off at a run, heading down the hill through the dense woodland. Lizards could attack at any moment—he knew that from his last visit. Max kept a careful lookout as he shoved his way through the waist-high grass. The slightest flash of scaly skin, and he'd be ready to swerve away.

As the camp drew nearer and nearer, Max began to get a funny feeling. Nothing had jumped out at him, and the ground seemed peaceful. All the same, the hairs on the back of his neck were prickling, as if something was following him.

He glanced behind him quickly, making sure he wasn't being followed.

But there was nothing there.

I'm going crazy, he thought.

Just then, he heard a faint rustling in the trees. He looked up—right into the pointy face of a bright green snake, dangling from a low branch!

The stalking reptile hadn't been behind him. It had been ABOVE him! It opened its jaws wide and lunged straight at him.

Max dodged out of the way just in time and fell, sprawling, on the ground. He scrambled to his feet and ran down the hillside as fast as he could go.

If he'd been full-size, he could have cupped the snake in his hands. But shrunken down as he was, the snake was gigantic, the size of a fallen tree trunk. It chased him easily, slithering from one low-hanging branch to the next.

Max desperately searched for a spot with no overhanging branches, but there was none. The nearest clear spot was the bug camp, and that was still far away.

The snake lunged again and again as Max ran. Each time, Max barely managed to avoid its pointy fangs. It would gulp him down in a second if it caught him.

The camp was getting closer. For a moment, Max thought he might make it. He strained to run even faster—and that was when disaster struck. His foot skidded on a damp patch of moss, and he felt his legs give way. Then he was on his back, helpless.

The snake's lean face loomed above him, blotting out the light. *This is it*, Max thought. *I'm finished.*

"You don't look like much," it whispered. "I probably won't even notice you going down my throat. Still, waste not, want not."

Then, suddenly, the snake hissed angrily and backed away. A black-and-yellow shape zoomed through the air like a fighter plane and stung it in the side. A giant hornet! Another one shot toward the snake, then another and another, until there were ten of them. They swarmed around the snake, diving in, stinging, and flying away.

"Go, Battle Bugs!" Max yelled. He punched the air. Buzz had come through with serious backup just in time!

The giant hornet commander broke formation with the others and made a perfect

landing by Max's side. "No time to explain now. Climb on."

"Good to see you, too, Buzz!" Max grinned.

He threw a leg over the hornet's back and grabbed on to the tough, spiky hairs that grew there. Buzz's wings became a blur as she lifted off from the ground in a stomach-lurching rush.

The snake tried one last time to make a wild lunge for Max, but Buzz was much faster and swerved easily out of the snake's strike path.

Max looked over his shoulder to see the snake writhing in agony as the hornet squadron drove their stings home. It retreated back up the hill, obviously too badly hurt to give chase.

"What *was* that snake?" Max wondered aloud. "I never even saw it coming."

"Better save the questions for Barton!" Buzz shouted. "He asked me to fly as high up as I could and try to summon you with my buzzing. I'm glad it worked. We need your help." Buzz flew up and away from the ground, far from where any reptiles could reach. "We've seen some strange things around the camp. Barton says we need your human brain to make sense of it. It's a good thing we found you in time."

Buzz flew the very relieved Max down into the clearing. The bug camp was surrounded by a circular wall with termite-mound towers set around it, dividing the wall into segments, like on a castle. Inside there were piles of debris for the bugs to live in, along with decaying logs, burrows, odd rocks, and piles of rotting food in the corners—just how they liked it!

"Can't stay and chat," Buzz said. "Gotta get back to the others. See you later!" With that, she flew off to rejoin her squadron.

Max watched the bugs work to build their camp. Now that he had a better look, he could see that it was far from finished.

Then he saw a familiar, gigantic shape emerge. It was Barton, the titan beetle and leader of the Battle Bugs. Max saluted as the huge bug came lumbering to his side.

"Welcome back, Max. You couldn't have come at a better time."

"I almost didn't make it at all! There was a snake!"

"It's not the first," Barton said darkly. "I need your brains, Max. My soldiers have seen many reptiles over the last few days— reptiles that we cannot explain." Max hadn't known that a titan beetle could sigh. "After your last visit, I had hoped we were safe. But the war goes on. I had to ask Buzz to try and call you back."

Max got ready to put his brains to work. "Where are the reptiles coming from?"

"It seems . . . from nowhere."

"The snake that attacked me was in the trees." Now that he wasn't being chased by the thing, Max found he was able to recall it clearly. "It was bright green, not very big for a snake, with an odd sort of face. Long and narrow, like a wedge."

"It must have been a long-nosed vine snake," Barton said. "We've tangled with them before. Snakes don't usually go after bugs like us, but General Komodo has obviously struck a deal with them. The long-nosed vine snakes look just like plants, so we can hardly see them at all when they hide in the trees. Until they strike."

"So they're using camouflage!" Max said.

"Exactly," rumbled Barton. "Which means one thing. They could be hiding *anywhere*."

MEETING THE TROOPS

"This changes everything," Max said. "If we can't see the reptiles until they're right on top of us, how are we going to defend ourselves?"

Barton began to pace back and forth. If he'd been a human being, Max thought, he'd have had his hands behind his back and a stern look on his face. "So far, they haven't launched an all-out attack. But it can only be a matter of time."

"Wait," said Max, confused. "How did the snakes even get over here? I thought the bugs were safe from the reptiles now. The river was supposed to act as a barrier, right?" On his last visit, the bugs had destroyed the path across the river. Everyone had celebrated, thinking they were safe. Obviously, all that had changed.

"General Komodo's troops must have found another way to reach us!" Barton said, snapping his mandibles together in anger. "Our enemy has learned from his mistakes, Max. He is sly. Why do you think he might have sent vine snakes so close to our camp, instead of launching a full-scale attack?"

Max thought for a minute. "Because of their camouflage, they could be spies!"

"I think you're right," Barton said. "He wants to know everything about our camp, especially all the weak points. Only then will he launch his attack."

Barton didn't sound worried by the idea. In fact, he sounded like he was looking forward to it.

"You have something up your sleeve, don't you?" Max asked.

"Hmm. What is a 'sleeve'?"

"I mean, you're prepared for Komodo's forces."

Barton nodded his huge head, nearly knocking Max over with his antennae. "Come this way," he said proudly. "It's time to inspect the troops."

He led Max down a ramp into an open area. It reminded Max of a fairground. Lined up in front of them, not moving a muscle, were ranks of reddish-yellow beetles. Just past them were ranks of copper-brown fire ants, and bringing up the rear was a troop of unusual spiders. Max grinned in excitement when he realized they were the same kind that he'd seen spinning the golden webs back at his family's campsite. Now maybe he'd learn what the spiders were.

"Soldiers!" Barton boomed. "Present . . . ARMS!"

To Max's amazement, the beetles in the front rank spun around and hoisted their bottoms into the air. The fire ants shoved their abdomens out, showing their stingers. The spiders each loosed a line of gleaming golden web.

"Impressive, aren't they?" Barton said. "Komodo won't know what hit him!"

"They're, um, very scary," said Max, wondering what exactly was supposed to be dangerous about a beetle's backside.

Barton must have noticed his confusion, because he bellowed to one of the beetles. "You there! Soldier! Name and rank?"

"Dungworth, SIR!" squeaked the beetle. "Sergeant and bombardier, SIR!"

Max managed not to laugh.

"This is Max, our military adviser. Show him what you're armed with. The rest of you, stand back!"

Everyone scurried out of the way.

The little beetle stood stock still, concentrating hard. Suddenly—FATOOM. An amazing blast of scalding steam shot out of his bottom.

Max coughed and waved a hand in front of his face. The vapor had reached his eyes, and it stung!

"Boiling acid!" Barton said. "Just let the reptiles get some of that in their faces, and they'll be sorry!"

Wow! Max thought. "What are the spiders?"

"Ah. Those are the golden orb weavers.

Splendid, all of them. Build some of the stickiest webs you could wish for."

Max filed the name away in his memory. *Golden orb weaver.* The name seemed rare and special, like the spider itself.

"Hey!" came a call from behind him. "Max! How are you doing, short stuff?" It was Spike, the emperor scorpion, waving his pincers happily.

"Max was just finishing his troop inspection," said Barton coolly.

"Yes, sir," Spike said, sounding embarrassed. "Sorry, sir. Didn't mean to interrupt."

"Good to see you, too, Spike!" Max said. He bumped his fist against Spike's outstretched pincer. "Commander Barton?

Since Spike and I made such a good team . . ."

"You'd like to work together again," Barton finished. "Of course. Spike, give Max a tour of the camp. Then get started on the spy problem. I want results!"

"Yes, sir!" they chorused.

"Dismissed!" bellowed Barton.

The organized ranks of bugs dissolved into a scuttling mass as they all clambered over one another, hurrying off to their assigned tasks.

Spike showed Max around the new and improved Battle Bug camp and the wall that surrounded it. "We got the termites to build most of it, since they're good at that sort of thing. They're not really soldiers like us, they're builders . . . Hey! Watch where you're going!"

"Sorry," grumbled a short, fat termite as it dodged between Spike's legs.

"Sentry towers are here and here," Spike explained, pointing. "Emergency food stores here . . . spider burrows here . . . this is where we'll set up the web walls if they try sending flying lizards at us."

"It's impressive," Max said. "It would be a shame if you had to abandon it and start again."

Spike jabbed his stinger at the huge triangular shadow blocking out half of the sky. "See Fang Mountain up there? Nothing but a spider could climb up those steep sides. We were counting on it to block the reptiles." He shook his head. "But they're still coming. I don't know how."

Max sat down on a white, domed object, which proved to be half a reptile egg that one of the bugs had brought back as a trophy. "Barton said they sent spies over."

"I've seen them! Vine snakes, mostly!"

Max racked his brains. "We have to figure out how they're coming in! If they've found a secret entrance, then the whole island is under threat. They could bring their entire army here and we'd never know . . ." He leapt to his feet. "I've got an idea."

Spike scuttled back and forth on all his legs, excited. "Yeah?"

"Maybe if we could catch a spy in the act, we could persuade it to talk!"

"That's brilliant," Spike said. "Make 'em tell us! But . . . uh . . . how would we catch 'em in the first place?"

"I know just who to ask. Come on! Let's go and find Webster."

Max hopped onto Spike's back, and they rode out of the main fortress gate, where two fire ants saluted them. Max knew Webster liked to lurk around the edge of forest clearings, so he rode Spike up to the tree line and searched for any telltale trap-doors Webster might have made.

Ten minutes later, he was getting worried. "Where is he? It's not like him to— WHOA!"

Webster was suddenly there in front of them, popping out of the ground like a jack-in-the-box. "M-M-Max! Hello!" he whispered.

"Hi Webster! You scared me!"

"Oh! I'm sorry!" Timidly, Webster began to creep back under his mat-like trapdoor of soil and plant debris. It always amazed Max that a spider who looked so scary could be so shy and quiet. It must've come from spending so long underground by himself in his tiny burrow.

"No, wait. It's good to see you! I need your help."

Webster hesitated.

Max patiently explained the situation. Webster had been really helpful the last time he was on Bug Island, and Max hoped he would be again. "I need you to make a trip wire," he said. "One long piece of silk running all around the camp, from tree to tree. Can you do that?"

"I think so," Webster said, wiggling his spinnerets.

"Good. Stick acorn shells halfway across each section."

"I don't get it," Spike moaned. "One little bit of spider silk isn't going to stop anyone."

Max grinned. "It's an early warning system! If any of the reptile spies try to get in, they'll touch the silk thread and the acorn shell will rattle. Then we'll know where they are."

Spike cheered. "We're going to beat the spies at their own sneaky game!"

SNEAKY SPIES

Max and Spike lay in wait, watching the acorn shells for the slightest sign of a tremor. From this distance, Webster's silk trip wire was almost invisible. A reptile spy wouldn't be able to see a thing.

"This dugout's a perfect hiding place," Max whispered to Spike, giving him a pat on his armored body. "I don't know how you dug it so fast."

"We emperor scorpions are pretty good diggers," Spike explained modestly. "We burrow for our food. Are you sure this is deep enough? I can burrow some more if you want."

"It's fine. Sshh!"

It was a bit like being in a trench from one of the old wars he'd read about, Max thought. The waiting was driving him crazy. The sun caught the silk wire for a second and it gleamed like a silver cable. Webster had carefully spun it just above the ground, which would alert them to any reptile intruder. Even a vine snake would have to drop down to ground level to approach the camp, because there was no tree cover in the clearing.

"This is fun," said Spike loudly, and Max had to hush him again.

It was exciting, he had to admit. But it wasn't quite the camping trip Max had expected when he and his parents set off that morning!

The excitement didn't last, however. Time passed slowly. Spike started humming and clicking his pincers. Nothing disturbed the trip wire. There were no shouts or alarm buzzes from the camp.

Max had the gloomy thought that a hidden reptile spy might have seen Webster setting the trip wire. They might be laughing at him and his clever plan right now.

At least it's nice and sunny, he thought.

In the next moment, thunder boomed in the distance. The sky darkened and began to cloud over. Max rolled his eyes. *That'll teach me!*

Minutes later, the rain began to fall. When you were this small, rain wasn't just annoying, it was downright dangerous. Raindrops fell like big boulders of water, bursting like hand grenades. When a drop came down next to Max, it drenched him as if a bucket of water had been flung over him. Miserably, he wrung out his sleeves.

Spike helpfully picked up a leaf and held it over their heads like an umbrella. The falling water boomed and splashed like kettledrums.

"This plan isn't very fun anymore," Spike grumbled.

"You said it," agreed Max.

He decided to tell Spike to pack up and head back to the camp. The reptiles had most likely returned to Reptile Island and were sheltering from the rain, while the bugs got caught in the downpour.

"Come on. We might as well . . ."

He stopped.

The nearest acorn shell was twitching. Then it fell to the ground.

Something had broken the wire!

"Spike!" he whispered, pointing.

"I see it. Something's breaking into the camp."

"Let's go. Stay low."

Max and Spike crept stealthily across the forest floor in the direction of the broken silk. Spike kept his stinger lowered, so as not to be seen.

They soon reached the exact place where the silk had snapped. Max was alert, looking all around for the slightest sign of a vine snake or crawling lizard. But he saw nothing.

"There's no one here," Spike said, sounding baffled.

"Just because we can't see anything doesn't mean there's no one here," Max reminded him. "The reptiles are sneaky, remember."

Max nudged Spike back toward the bug camp. They moved in, very slowly. *If I were a reptile spy*, Max thought, *this is where I'd go.*

"There!" Spike hissed.

Max squinted. "I can't see anything."

"By the edge of that rock, see?"

Max narrowed his eyes. Then he saw them: two lizards, scrambling up from the leafy forest floor onto the rock that Spike had mentioned. They had eyes like armored turrets, which swiveled around in their heads and pointed in different directions. *What perfect spies they must make*, Max thought.

His mouth fell open as he watched. The lizards had been brownish-green, almost impossible to see among the fallen leaves and moss. But as they climbed on to the

gray rock, their skins changed color until they were as gray as the rock itself.

Soon they looked just like bumpy bulges on the rock surface. If they hadn't climbed onto the rock, Max might never have seen them at all. He could barely make them out now.

"Chameleons," he said. "I've heard of them. They usually change their color to match how they're feeling. These two must be doing it on purpose to hide."

"No wonder General Komodo sent them!" Spike said angrily. "Talk about stealthy. At least you can see a vine snake when it falls out of its tree. How can you spot a lizard that changes color?"

"Let's get closer. We need to hear what they're planning."

The rain was falling heavily now, lashing down all around them. Max was soaked to the skin. Thunder rumbled and boomed so often that it hid the sound of Spike trampling through the leaves. At least the chameleons wouldn't hear them sneaking up behind.

They came close enough to hear the two lizards talking in quiet, slithery voices.

"Ssso, Dagger, the main gate is defended by fire antsss, is it? What are those brown beetlesss?"

"I do not know them, Cloak. They are new. Where are the spidersss?"

"Hiding, no doubt. They are cowardsss who lurk while others fight . . ."

Max leaned in close to Spike's armorplated head. "They're scoping out our defenses!" he whispered.

Cloak and Dagger sat and looked over the camp for a while, swiveling their eyes around like surveillance cameras. The rain was coming down even harder now, battering the camp, sending bugs scurrying to find shelter. Max was glad for the heavy rain, though; it would be making it harder for the chameleons to snoop.

"The bugs suspect nothing," Dagger hissed. "General Komodo will be most pleased."

Max knew *that* name all too well. Komodo, the fearsome leader of the reptile forces, was a monitor lizard. He towered over his troops, as ravenous as he was cruel.

"When he hears how ill-prepared the bugs are, he will decide to lead the attack personally!" gloated Cloak.

Max strained to hear what they were saying. He just caught the words ". . . ready for a noon raid . . ." before a tremendous clap of thunder drowned out the chameleon's words.

Dagger said something about "mountain lizards" and "collared lizards," but again, thunder crashed overhead. The chameleons chuckled hoarsely, gloating over the bugs they would catch unawares.

"I've heard enough," Spike said, grinding his pincers in anger. "Let's go to Barton right now!"

"Not yet!" Max whispered urgently. "We need to find out where they're coming from, remember?"

"Oh, yeah. Maybe we can ambush them before they get to us."

Max expected the chameleon spies to go back the way they'd come, but, to his surprise, they didn't. Instead, they headed off toward the edge of the clearing and made their way into the forest in the direction of Fang Mountain.

Max rode after them on Spike, keeping his distance so they wouldn't be seen. Heading for Fang Mountain didn't make sense at all. There was no way General Komodo could lead an army over the mountain range. Maybe the chameleons had seen him and Spike and were now leading them into a trap? Any moment now, a dozen vine snakes might drop out of the trees.

But there was no ambush. The chameleons kept going all the way to the foot of Fang Mountain. The sky overhead was now the gray-black shade of a burnt camping pot, and the peals of thunder were louder than ever.

There were no more trees here. A sheer

cliff face loomed over them. The rock was streaming wet with rain. Max was baffled. Even chameleons couldn't climb up a surface like that.

He peered through the curtain of falling water. And then he saw it, what the chameleons were heading toward—a jagged crack part way up the rock wall, as if a huge pick had swung down and split it. The lizards wriggled through and disappeared.

"Can you get us in there?" Max asked Spike.

"No problem!"

Spike climbed a little pile of rocks and edged his way into the crack.

"Wow," Max said, as he saw what was on the other side. "That explains everything.

Looks like Fang Mountain wasn't as protective as everyone thought."

The crack in the rock wall opened onto a thin, twisting mountain pass. On both sides, rocky cliffs rose up, looking crumbly and loose. The chameleons were already scrambling around a distant turn and vanishing out of sight.

"Hurry! After them!"

Spike did his best to follow, but it was no good. He didn't know the safe places to walk, and several times the wet ground kept sliding away underneath him in a rattling cascade. It was getting hard to see anything at all in this storm.

Spike was halfway up a steep, rocky pathway, when a bright blue flash lit up the sky. A snaking trail of lightning ripped into the mountain wall. Earth and rocks, torn loose by the blast, showered down on them.

Max froze in horror as a boulder came tumbling toward his head!

LANDSLIDE!

"Landslide!" Max yelled. Spike lurched forward, and the boulder whammed down right where Max's head had been.

Pebbles and chunks of rock rained down on them. Spike barely seemed to notice. "The little rocks don't hurt," he shouted back. "They just bounce off your body plating."

"I don't HAVE any body plating! I'm human, remember?"

"Oh, yeah! Sorry, I forgot!" Spike picked up speed and raced toward the valley opening.

A huge muddy clump came loose from high above and tumbled down. Max glanced up and yelled for Spike to swerve sideways. The scorpion banked up the side of the valley like a stunt driver swerving around a tight corner.

Debris showered them as the boulder landed just behind them. It could have squashed Spike flat, body armor or no body armor.

"It's getting worse," Max shouted. "The cliff walls are crumbling."

They dashed down the valley through the pounding rain, dodging out of the way of falling rocks. The hail of pebbles and rock fragments was turning into a full-scale avalanche. The exit from the pass was still a long way off.

With a sickening feeling, Max realized they weren't going to make it.

Suddenly, Spike spotted a gap in the rock. "A cave!" he bellowed. "Hold on tight. Keep your head down. I'm going in!"

His heart hammering, Max pressed himself down against Spike's back. The scorpion wrestled his way through the tight opening and into a pitch-black cave. Rocks scraped against Max's back, nearly pulling him off. He clung to Spike with all his strength.

Behind them, the last scrap of daylight vanished. The cave mouth was buried under falling rocks.

"That was too close." Max panted.

"We'd better stay in here until the storm passes," said Spike. "It's too dangerous out there."

Max felt the rocks blocking the cave. They were packed tight.

"It doesn't look like we have much of a choice."

They sat in darkness for what felt like hours, listening to the rumble of falling stones and the patter of falling rain. Max ground his teeth. *I have to warn Barton*, he thought.

The attack's coming tomorrow and they don't even know!

It was a long time before the storm finally cleared. "I think we can get going now," Max said. He gave the rocks a push, but they didn't budge. "Uh, Spike . . . I think this is a job for you."

"Coming through!" Spike yelled happily. His great pincers swung forward like bucket cranes. He grasped a rock in each one and heaved. As they gave way, sunlight streamed in through the hole he'd made.

Feeling much better, Max scraped some of the smaller stones away until he was able to pull himself out. His clothes were *filthy*. When his mom saw, she'd have a fit.

The valley was calm now. Pools of

rainwater glittered in the sunlight. The air smelled of freshly dug earth and moist rocks.

Max looked down the pass, thinking about the reptile army that would soon come swarming through. Then he noticed something strange. The cliff walls had only crumbled away near the bottom. Why hadn't they given way higher up?

He looked up and found his answer. The roots of trees, along with a tangled array of vines and creepers, had grown over the upper part of the cliffs long ago. They lay like a greenish-brown net, keeping the cliffs from giving way any further.

"See that?" he told Spike. "All that green stuff saved our lives. If that hadn't been there, we'd have been buried alive!"

"Don't wanna think about it." Spike shuddered. "Let's get back to camp."

To Max's dismay, they found the bug camp half collapsed. One of the wall sections was completely gone, along with its bombardier-beetle tower. Legs waved feebly as bugs were dug out of the wreckage.

"Did the reptiles do this?" Max asked a nearby fire ant, who was lugging a leaf five times her size.

"No!" the ant said. "This is storm damage!"

Max and Spike exchanged looks. "Phew. Thought they'd attacked early," the scorpion said.

Barton appeared on the battlements, with Buzz hovering alongside. "Max! Good to see you're safe. I was about to send a search party." Buzz zoomed down to give Max a lift to the top of the encircling wall.

Max quickly told Barton and Buzz all about the hidden mountain pass and the sneaky chameleon spies. "The lizards are planning an attack tomorrow at noon," he finished.

Barton summoned a fire ant officer. "I want all bugs working double time to rebuild the fortress," he ordered. "Max, I want you to join me, Buzz, Spike, and Webster in the war room."

Barton's "war room" turned out to be the inside of a hollow log. Some helpful wasps had built a model of Bug Island out of chewed paper pulp. Barton pointed to it with his antennae as he spoke.

"Buzz, take your hornet squadron for a flyby of the mountain pass. I want regular air patrols, understood?"

"Roger that, sir."

Max, Barton, Spike, and Webster discussed battle plans. Barton was obviously counting on Max to come up with a brilliant idea, but he just couldn't think of one. Spike suggested loading the hornets up with bombardier beetles and dropping them on the lizards like bombs, but Barton refused: "They are soldiers, Spike, not ammunition!"

"We could always send the termites in," Spike joked.

"What good would *they* be?"

"Once the lizards have eaten 'em all, they'll be too fat to move."

"That will do, Spike," said Barton darkly. "We all do our part, even the termites."

"Sorry, sir," mumbled Spike.

As for Webster, he barely spoke at all, and his only suggestion was: "We could all hide under a big rock," to which Barton didn't even bother responding.

Max felt sorry for Webster. After all, without his help they never would have known the chameleon spies were there. Maybe there was some other way they could use webbing . . .

"The golden orb weavers!" Max yelled. "Of course! They can weave sticky webs between the two sides of the mountain pass." He remembered seeing the golden orb weaver do that when he was camping. "That'll slow the lizards down."

"Excellent," Barton said. "Spike, let's assemble the golden orb weavers and put Max's plan into action."

Max hung back while the others prepared to leave camp. He looked around for Webster, who had retreated into the depths of the log. "Webster, I have another idea— only to be used in case of emergency."

"What is it, M-Max?" Webster asked.

"Webs are amazing, but some spiders are good at digging, too. Can you and your trapdoor spider friends make some burrows in the middle of the camp?"

"I think so," whispered Webster. "How many?"

"As many as you can. Dozens would be good. Hundreds would be better."

"What for?" asked Barton.

"Emergency defense," said Max. "Which I'm hoping we won't need."

FANG MOUNTAIN BATTLE

Max spent the night curled up in an empty egg casing, which was soft, rubbery, and comfortable. In the morning, Barton prodded him awake. "It's invasion day. Time to head out to the front line and meet with Spike."

Soon they were climbing up into the crevice at the bugs' end of the mountain pass. They headed up a pile of recently fallen debris. It reached high enough to give a good view of the mountain pass, but wasn't too sheer for Max to climb. He felt dizzy with excitement. The lizards were coming . . . but the bugs were ready for them.

The golden orb weavers had been hard at work all night. Hundreds of webs, as golden as honey and twice as sticky, now blocked the pass. They looked like nets stretched tight between the two cliff faces. As a second line of defense, Barton had stationed the bug battalions behind them. Fire ants and stag beetles waited to unleash the might of the Battle Bugs on any lizard that blundered into the webbing.

"Is it noon yet?" Spike asked impatiently, twitching his stinger.

Max looked up at the sun, which was high in the sky. "Almost."

"Do you think they're still coming?"

"They will come," said Barton gravely.

Just then, Max heard the familiar sound of Buzz's wings beating frantically. The hornet came in for a fast landing, slamming down on the gravelly ground next to them. "The lizards are on their way through the mountain!" she gasped. "I just saw them heading out. There are dozens of them."

"Brace yourselves!" Barton roared to the troops.

Just then, Max heard a scurrying, hammering sound like many different drums pounding at once. He knew immediately it was the oncoming lizard army. Their footfalls echoed through the mountain pass.

The invading group rounded the corner, and Max got his first good look at them. The front rank was made up of burly lizards with rows of spines down their backs. *Mountain lizards*, Max thought. Close behind them came large-headed lizards with striking, collar-like bands of color around their necks. The horned mountain lizards stampeded up the pass. They saw the webs but charged forward anyway.

As the lizards barged into the webs, sticky strands tangled around their eyes and mouths. They pressed forward, trying to break through. Some of the webs tore under

the weight of all the lizard bodies pressing against them, but the main barrier held.

More lizards charged into the backs of the stuck ones, like a pileup on the highway. The farther the ones at the front were shoved into the web, the more hopelessly entangled they became. Their heads and feet were masses of webbing.

It's working! Max thought excitedly. *They can't see and they can barely move.*

"Buzz!" boomed Barton. "Launch the hornet squadrons. Those lizards are packed tight down there, and they're stuck fast. Should be easy targets."

"Yes, sir!" Buzz said.

The hornets zoomed in, raining down stings on the helpless lizards. "Stay away from the webbing!" Max yelled. If the bold hornets were caught in their own side's defenses, they'd be sitting ducks.

Chaos and confusion swept through the lizard ranks. They had been a proud army, on their way to ambush a helpless foe. Now, suddenly, they were blinded, attacked from all sides, and struggling to move. The golden orb weavers kept on spinning, adding more and more webs to the barricade.

Max grinned, but the grin suddenly faded as he saw a fearsome, bulging-eyed lizard hacking and slashing its way through the golden webs. The creature's body was covered with thorny spikes, just like the sharp prickles on a rose bush. Like a nightmarish living cactus, it clambered over the unmoving, tangled lizards and made straight for the main webbing barricade.

"Max, do you recognize that creature?" Barton asked.

"It's a thorny devil lizard," Max told him. "It's using its spikes to rip the webs away. The orb weavers are in danger—we have to warn them!"

Before Barton could stop him, Max took off running down the pile of rubble. He scrambled to the base of the ravine and headed right for the front line.

The thorny devil lizard was slowly plowing through the webs like a lawnmower through thick grass. The other lizards advanced behind it, letting it clear the path for them. Their eyes gleamed with hunger. Some of them even snapped at Buzz's hornets as they swept in to attack.

The orb weavers were between Max and the advancing lizards, still spinning their webs!

Max ran closer, wading into the web-strewn mess that the spiders had made of the ravine floor. "Retreat!" he shouted up to them.

"But we're needed!" shrilled an orb weaver.

"The webs can't stop them now. You need to let the stag beetles take over!"

The lizards were almost through. The orb weavers hurriedly skittered away, looking glad to fall back and leave the fighting to sturdier bugs.

Now Max just had to get *himself* out of the way. If he stuck around, he could get eaten or even caught in a cloud of boiling beetle acid. He turned to run but his feet wouldn't move. His legs were caught in a tangle of sticky golden ropes. He'd waded farther into the orb weavers' webs than he'd thought, and now he was trapped.

Max grabbed his right leg with both hands and heaved. The webs made a sucking, stretching noise, but stayed stuck fast to his feet. It felt like he was standing in a massive wad of chewing gum.

From up ahead came the *thoom, thoom, thoom* of heavy lizard footsteps. The thorny devil lizard was tearing its way through the last few webs. It peered down through the webbed barrier at the struggling Max and smiled slowly.

"A little soft bug with no shell," it said. "Nice little morsel for me. Then I can tuck into the main course of Battle Bugs!"

The lizard was so close now, Max could smell its meaty breath. One web after another was torn away, and he still couldn't move.

The thorny devil ripped down the last golden web. "GOT YOU!"

Just as it opened its jaws and lunged, there was a whirr of wings from overhead. It was Barton, flying in with Spike in his grasp. Barton dropped the emperor scorpion right in front of the lizard.

Max gasped in surprise. It looked like Barton's wing had finally healed—and just in time!

"Pick on someone your own size!" Spike roared, and jammed his stinger into the lizard's open mouth. As it howled in pain, Spike quickly scissored through the webs with his pincers, setting Max free.

"Am I glad to see you, big guy," Max gasped. He climbed on top of Spike and they dashed back along the pass, swerving out of the way of the oncoming force of stag beetles, with Barton following overhead.

As they scrambled down the ravine, they heard a roar from behind them.

Max looked over his shoulder. What he saw made his blood turn as cold as any reptile's. Over the heads of the oncoming lizard army loomed the fierce and terrifying figure of General Komodo.

KOMODO APPEARS

Facing Komodo was the closest Max would ever get to looking a live dinosaur in the eye. A gigantic monitor lizard, Komodo towered over the other reptiles, glaring down at the bugs. He hissed, making some of the smaller beetles quiver in fear. A forked, snakelike tongue appeared, flickering out and back.

"Was this seriously your plan, Barton?" Komodo roared. "A few pathetic scraps of web were supposed to stop my army? It took only one lizard to tear them down!"

Yeah, but we took out dozens of lizards first, Max thought. Those lizards were still tangled in webbing, struggling feebly.

"This island will be mine before sunset," Komodo gloated. "It will be Bug Island no more. I will rename it Komodo's Palace! Your pathetic bug warriors will provide our victory feast."

Barton swaggered through his troops toward Komodo, showing them he wasn't afraid.

"Are you sure you're a lizard?" he called. "Because you're puffing yourself up like a toad. I'll have to let some of that hot air out of you!"

The beetles laughed, and Komodo snarled.

"My spies have found out all about your fortress. I will tear it down myself."

"You'll have to get past me first," Barton said. He slowly opened his huge pincers and snapped them together with a sharp crack.

Komodo flinched—and everybody saw it. A murmur ran through the ranks on both sides.

Barton beckoned Max to sit on his back. Together they headed to the very front of the battle line, where the stag beetles stood braced to charge, facing off against a row of mountain lizards.

"Battle Bugs! Attack!" shouted Barton.

The brave beetles charged. The army swept down the valley like a scuttling black river. It crashed into the advancing lizards.

The lizards snapped their jaws and fought, but the bugs' sheer numbers overwhelmed them. The stag beetles used their strong pincers to nip at the lizards' legs, pulling them off balance. Barton yelled orders, telling the next wave of stag beetles where to strike.

The valley rang with the sounds of furious battle: beetles buzzed, lizards hissed, and the two commanders yelled orders and encouragement. Komodo bellowed at his troops to stop letting the bugs walk all over them: "Just eat them, you fools!"

Barton yelled to the stag beetles to hold the line: "Onward, Battle Bugs! Pull them down!"

No matter what the lizards did, the bugs kept coming. The lizards' problem was that they were just too close to the ground, shuffling forward on all fours. It was easy for the living carpet of stag beetles to rush over them. While one beetle pinched a lizard's mouth shut so that it couldn't bite, others would pull its legs out from under it. Soon the lizard would be struggling on its back, unable to move. That made it an easy target for Spike's sting. The orb weavers waited patiently, twiddling their legs, preparing to wrap up lizard prisoners in strong spider silk.

"Over there!" Max pointed. "That little beetle's in trouble!"

Barton raced over to where a lizard was whipping its head to the left and right. A small stag beetle, anxious to prove how brave he was, had taken on the lizard by himself. Now he was hanging on to the lizard's lower jaw for dear life.

"I'm fi-i-ine, sir!" squeaked the beetle. "I can handle him!"

Barton grabbed the beetle in his pincers, pulled him away, and dropped him safely to one side. The lizard lunged at the fallen beetle, trying to swallow him, but Barton

swung his colossal pincers and knocked the lizard sprawling.

Max directed Barton to the other side of the valley, where a group of mountain lizards were breaking through the battle line. With Barton lending his strength, the stag beetles soon forced them back.

"We're beating them," Max said with a grin. *This is going a lot better than I expected*, he thought to himself.

"Yes, but they're too stupid to know when they're beaten," Barton said. "We need to break their will to fight. But how?"

Max thought about it. "Unleash the fire ants! Their stings hurt like anything. They'll get the lizards to turn tail and run."

Barton lifted his head and buzzed so loudly, Max had to cover his ears.

The fire ant legions poured into the valley. They were a terrifying sight, their copper-red bodies gleaming in the sun, their mandibles gaping and ready to bite, their stingers packed full of venom. One fire ant on its own was nothing to be scared of, but hundreds and hundreds of them together with their red-hot stings were enough to make any lizard think twice.

The ants rushed between the much larger stag beetles, plowing into the lizards and stinging wherever they could. Lizards reared up, moaning in pain, with red sting marks on their noses and bellies. A few of them, stung from head to tail, had had enough and turned to flee.

"Go on," yelled Max. "Run! Back to your own island!" The fire ants cheered.

"Foolish bugs," roared General Komodo. "You think we would give up that easily?" He lumbered forward. "Collared lizards! Execute battle plan RAPTOR."

All at once, the collared lizards rose up and stood on their hind legs. Max remembered hearing they could do that, but he'd never seen it happen in real life.

The effect was stunning. Now that the lizards loomed above the bugs, the beetles couldn't swarm over them. The fire ants couldn't sting their faces and bellies. The lizards were free to stride forward through the beetles, snapping and chomping wher-ever they liked.

In seconds, the Battle Bug victory turned into a disaster. Max saw fire ant soldiers snatched up by collared lizard jaws. Power-ful legs kicked stag beetles onto their backs, where they lay helpless, unable to turn right-side up again.

Komodo laughed, an ugly sound. More and more collared lizards came sprinting from behind—running on their hind legs, they were *fast*.

The front rank of bugs turned and ran. That was the worst thing that could have happened. The collared lizards swept down upon them. The fleeing bugs barged into their own rear guard, causing panic and total confusion.

"We're losing!" Spike shouted in despair. "Commander, what do we do?"

Barton turned to Max. "We need a new plan!"

Max shook his head. "It's no use. We have to retreat."

BATTLE BUGS
ATTACK!

"FALL BACK!" The cry went up from bug to bug, across the army.

The Battle Bugs ran as fast as they could. The narrow ravine was a choked mass of bugs, with insects scrambling over one another in their haste to get out.

The collared lizards chased after them,

laughing cruelly. "Don't bother running," one of them hissed. "You'll only die tired!"

Max jolted around on Barton's back. The collared lizards were only a few paces behind. He fought to keep his nerve at the terrifying sight. All around him, bugs were being knocked out of action. A few even got caught in the orb weaver webs, which had seemed like such a good idea before.

"Where do we retreat to?" called Spike as he banked up the side of the ravine.

"Back to camp!" Max yelled.

"No!" Barton told him in horror. "We can't lead the lizards there. They'll destroy it, and then the whole island will be theirs."

"We have no choice. It's an emergency."
And if Webster has done what I asked him,
Max thought, *leading them back to camp*
might be our only hope.

"I'm putting my trust in you, Max. I hope
you don't let me down."

They reached the end of the ravine. The
bugs poured out like a living waterfall. Now
that they were no longer trapped between
the cliff walls, they could spread out and run
freely. The lucky ones who could fly opened
their wing cases and took to the air. The
poor fire ants, who had been a proud fighting force that morning, had to run for their
lives through the foliage of the forest floor.

"When you reach camp, take to the trees
or to your burrows!" Barton shouted.

"Whatever you do, stay away from the lizards," added Max. "Leave the fortress to us."

Only minutes later, Max and Barton rode through a tiny gap in the camp wall. The termites had done a wonderful job of rebuilding it. The walls looked strong, the towers sturdy. Max just hoped Webster and his trapdoor spider friends had dug the burrows.

Most of the bugs vanished into the trees and down into their holes, as they'd been ordered to. Only Barton, Spike, Buzz, and a handful of fire ants and stag beetles were left to defend the camp. They stood on a raised, steep-sided mound overlooking the main courtyard.

General Komodo came crashing through

the trees. His bodyguard of fierce-looking lizards followed close behind him.

"Well, well, well. So this is Barton's mighty walled camp, is it? Nothing but mud and termite spit!" Komodo mocked.

"Come over here and say that!" Max shouted.

"Oh, I will . . . Now my victory is complete. Your forces are scattered. There is nothing to stop me from marching in and taking over."

"We *will* stop you!" Spike hollered.

Komodo laughed heartily. "Oh, please. As if you still have a chance!" Impatiently, he flicked his tail at the fortress. "Smash your way in," he told his guards.

The lizards scrabbled and clawed at the fortress wall, ripping chunks of it away, until they cleared a gap big enough to pass through. One by one, Komodo's forces slithered into the wide-open courtyard. Above, on their mound, Max and the others looked down at him. *Almost . . .* Max thought. *Keep coming . . .*

Before long, the fortress was filled up with lizards. They glanced around hungrily, waiting for Komodo's orders. He laughed. "You think you are safe up there, you pitiful bugs? I'll tear the whole place down to reach you if I have to!"

"Webster!" Max shouted. "NOW!"

He heard Webster respond with a battle

cry. The spider burst out from one of his trapdoors, right into the open courtyard where the lizards now stood!

But Webster was not alone. Hundreds of trapdoor burrows opened, all around the startled lizards. Crawling out of them came the bombardier beetles—*thousands* of them—and the lizards were trapped in the middle.

Komodo's eyes bulged with rage as he realized what was happening. The lizards were not only surrounded, but the beetles were right in among them. The reptiles didn't know what they were in for. But they were about to find out.

"Bombardier beetles, open fire!" Max yelled.

FATOOM FATOOM FATOOM, went the sound of the beetles' bottoms. A mass blast of boiling, burning acid steam engulfed the helpless lizards. They couldn't fight back because they were too busy screeching in pain.

FATOOM. A collared lizard rolled over, waving its legs. FATOOM. FATOOM. Lizards coughed and spluttered, unable to breathe. Some of them tried to escape by climbing the walls, but they were just too steep. FATOOM. General Komodo shrieked with rage, clawing at his eyes. "I can't see! *I'll get you for this, Barton!*"

The beetles kept firing like poisonous party poppers. Max cheered. "We warned you, Komodo! But you walked right into our trap!"

"General!" howled a mountain lizard. "How can we fight? We can't even *see*!"

"No excuses!" Komodo commanded. "Just eat them. We are lizards. It's what we do, you fool."

The lizard tried to obey, but he got a faceful of venom from Sergeant Dungworth and ran away screeching.

The lizards were beginning to pile back out through the hole they'd bashed in the wall.

"Well done, Max," said Barton. "Should we make them pay?"

"Oh, I think we should," Max said fiercely. "Battle Bugs! ATTACK!"

The bugs dived down from the mound into the battleground. Stag beetles and fire ants launched themselves into the attack, driving the disoriented lizards away. The damaged wall crumbled even more under the weight of dozens of lizards fighting to escape.

Barton lunged into the battle with his pincers and caught something thick and meaty. To Max's amazement, he saw it was General Komodo's tongue! Barton stretched it out, making the lizard bellow in agony, then let go.

"Get off my island!" Barton roared.

Shattered, blinded, and stung, the lizards were forced to flee. They made a quick exit, limping in confusion, heading back in the direction of the mountain pass.

Max stood in the battle-torn fortress,

watching them go. A cheer went up from all around.

"Victory!"

Spike patted Max on the shoulder with a foreleg. "Great plan. You're a hero, Max. Well done!"

BRAVE BUGS

Max leaned against the wall, gasping in relief. The Battle Bugs cheered, clicked their pincers, did victory dances, and broke open the nectar stores to celebrate. Injured soldier beetles shook each other by the claw, apparently unconcerned that they were bashed or bruised or missing one of their many legs!

Barton went from bug to bug, congratulating each one. "Well fought; well done, soldier; brave bugs, all. Good job."

"The lizards will be on their way through the mountain pass by now," said Buzz. "Shame we can't bring the whole thing down on their heads."

"Those bombardier beetles taught them a lesson they'll never forget!" Max grinned.

Spike fidgeted anxiously. He wasn't joining in the celebration like all the rest. Max had to ask him what was wrong.

"The lizards might be gone for now, but what if they come back?" Spike whispered. "They can come through Fang Mountain whenever they want. Next time, they'll be more prepared. They won't fall for the same trap twice."

Max frowned. The scorpion was right. As long as that pass stood open, Bug Island would never be safe.

There had to be something they could do. He thought carefully.

Then his face lit up. "Spike, you're a genius."

"Me?" Spike was baffled.

"You came up with the answer yourself, back in the war room. Send the termites in!"

Barton overheard. "I said there was to be no joking about the termites!"

"I'm not joking. I'm completely serious. Here's what we do . . ."

*   *   *

Back at the mountain pass, Max was relieved to see that the reptiles were nowhere in sight. That meant there was time to do the job he had in mind. Barton, Buzz, Webster, and Spike looked on, curious to see what he was planning.

The termites were gathered behind him, waiting for his instructions.

"You see where the rocks are crumbling at the top of the cliffs?" Max pointed up. "All those roots and vines and creepers are holding the cliff together."

"Yeah," said the termite foreman gruffly. "What about it?"

"Think your crew can chew through all that green stuff and cause a landslide?"

The termite foreman thought it over. "Piece of cake," he said. "We'll have it done in ten minutes. Come on, everybody! We have a job to do!"

The termites scurried up the cliffs, poured over the vines, and disappeared into the greenery above. The valley filled with the sound of thousands of pairs of tiny jaws munching.

Max waited. Soon the first tree root fell with a crash, then the next. A dusty shower of rocks followed. The net of vines holding the rockfall back began to sag. He grinned. *It's working!*

The termites chewed and chewed. Vine after vine snapped and fell, until with a sudden roar the whole cliffside gave way. The pass filled up with rocks, blocking it off completely.

"Nice job!" Max called as the dust settled. "The lizards won't be trying this route any time soon."

He checked his watch. *Two minutes and thirty-eight seconds: that was fast work!*

"Well done, termites!" said Barton.

The other bugs all congratulated the termites, too. Even Spike had to admit that they'd done well. The termites were surprised to find themselves treated like heroes, for once!

Max smiled. Then he felt something hot

in his pocket. He pulled it out and saw that it was the magnifying glass, glowing brightly.

"It must be time for me to go," Max told them all.

"Thanks for everything," Buzz said. "We'll be sure to call if we need you again."

"*When* we need you again," added Barton. "Somehow I don't think Komodo is going to give up."

"I'll be there!" Max promised. He said a hasty good-bye to his friends, saluted Barton, lifted the magnifying glass up to the sky, and looked through it.

Just like last time, Max felt a tugging sensation in the pit of his stomach, and wind whirled past him. It was like being vacuumed up into the sky—upside down and backward!

With a jolt, Max found himself back inside the family motor home, next to the open encyclopedia, exactly as he had been when he left. The clock on the microwave showed that only a few hours had passed— and his clothes were as clean as when he'd put them on that morning!

"Phew," he said. "Nice to be back."

He went outside and saw that the sky had darkened. His mom and dad were waiting by a huge campfire, ready with sticks and a bag of marshmallows.

"Nice to see you at last!" his dad laughed. "You've been reading that book for hours."

"It's my favorite book," said Max, honestly.

"Did you find out what that spider was?"

"I sure did. It was a golden orb weaver."

"Ooh," said his mom. "That's a pretty name, actually. For a *spider*, I mean."

Max thought back to the mountain pass, and how the golden orb weavers had slowed the lizard army down with their amazing sticky webs. What on earth would his parents say if they knew where he'd really been?

His dad passed him a marshmallow on a stick, ready for toasting. "You know, Max, I think this is going to be a camping trip to remember."

Max smiled. "I think you might be right!"

REAL LIFE BATTLE BUGS!

Golden Orb Weaver Spiders

The golden orb weaver gets its name not because of the color of the spider itself, but because of the yellow silk it uses to trap its prey. This sticky web glistens in the sun, making it look like shiny, gold thread.

Golden orb weaver spiders make some of the largest webs in the world. They can be over three feet in diameter. That's big enough to catch bats and small birds!

Bombardier Beetles

The bombardier beetle is one of nature's most fascinating bugs. Not many living creatures can boast an exploding backside, but the bombardier beetle certainly can!

The beetle has two small glands toward the rear of its abdomen; each contains a different liquid. When threatened, the beetle can mix the two together in what's known as its "explosion chamber." Then the beetle fires the dangerous mixture toward its unlucky victim. The liquid can reach a temperature of over 200 degrees!

Termites

Termites might look very similar to ants, but they're actually a species of cockroach! Termites live very different lives from any cockroach we might encounter. They are a social insect, dividing work between each other and looking after their young collectively.

Termites build elaborate nests made of chewed-up soil, mud, tree bark, and even animal poop in order to provide a protected home for their colony. The nests are usually found underground, but sometimes become so big that they grow several yards out of the ground, becoming termite mounds: the skyscrapers of the insect world.

THE ADVENTURE CONTINUES!

The Battle Bugs are facing peril from all sides. General Komodo has forged an alliance with insect-hungry birds—and with an elite fleet of poison dart frogs. While the birds attack from above, the poisonous frogs attack from below!

Max has a daring plan—but will it be enough?